MW01049596

MEET THE
PENGUINS!

by Daphne Pendergrass

Simon Spotlight

New York London Toronto Sydney New Delhi

SIMON SPOTLIGHT

An imprint of Simon & Schuster Children's Publishing Division
1230 Avenue of the Americas, New York, New York 10020
This Simon Spotlight paperback edition October 2014
Penguins of Madagascar © 2014 DreamWorks Animation L.L.C.
For information about special discounts for bulk purchases,
please contact Simon & Schuster Special Sales at 1-866-506-1949
or business@simonandschuster.com.
Designed by John Daly
Manufactured in the United States of America   0914 LAK
10 9 8 7 6 5 4 3 2 1
ISBN 978-1-4814-3734-9
ISBN 978-1-4814-3735-6 (eBook)

Shanghai

- More than twenty million people live in Shanghai, making it the largest city in China and one of the largest cities in the world. In fact, there are more people living in Shanghai than in many countries!

  - Shanghai sits on the Yangtze River, which is the third longest river in the world. The first is the Nile in Africa, and the second is the Amazon in South America.

    - Shanghai was nothing more than a small fishing village until 1842 when it became an international port.

Antarctica

- Antarctica isn't just cold, it's windy too! Winds can be as strong as 200 miles per hour.

  - The world's most southern active volcano, Mount Erebus, is found on Antarctica.

    - Even with all that ice, Antarctica is considered a desert since very little rain or snow falls there.

Congratulations!

Your mission to meet the penguins, their friends and foes, and explore their action-packed world is complete. As you can see, Skipper, Kowalski, Rico, and Private are not your average flightless birds. See you next time! Until then—high-one!

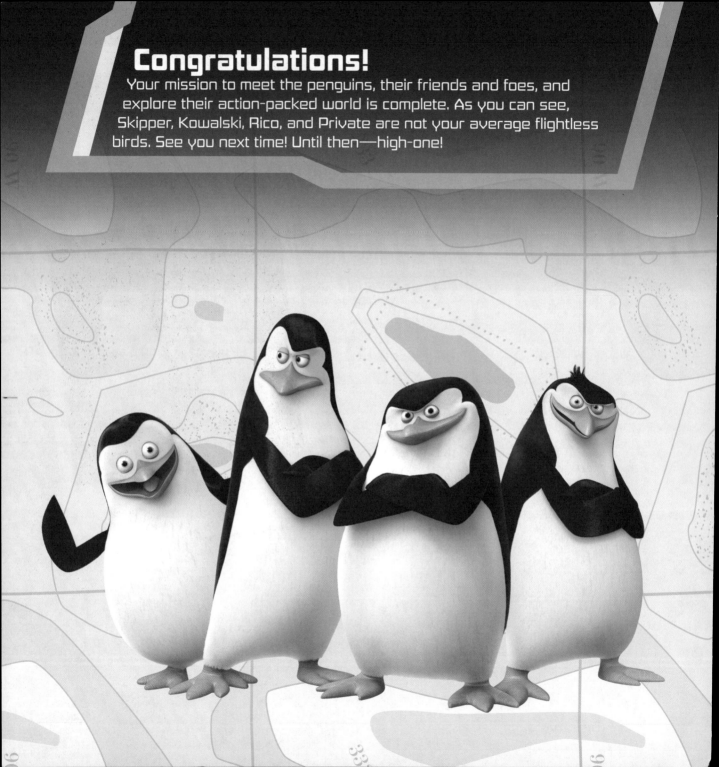

SKIPPER.
KOWALSKI.
RICO.
PRIVATE.

To the untrained eye they might look like four ordinary penguins, but this team is actually the elite-est of elite units, with unrivaled talents, unmatched abilities, and unquestionable results. So form your battle stance and aim for first class—it's time to meet Skipper and the boys!

SKIPPER, the Leader

A born leader, the man with the plan, Skipper can easily handle even the most difficult situation with a few words and a wave of his flipper. But Skipper isn't all business—he's very protective of his team, especially when it comes to Private, whom he raised from just an egg.

STRENGTHS

- Split-second decision making
- Remaining cool under pressure
- Formulating plans

Skipper Knows Best

"Never trust a Dutchman in a tulip fight."

"Canada is secretly training an army of Sasquatch."

"Hot dogs are, in fact, only 17 percent actual dog."

KOWALSKI, the Brains

Kowalski's talent lies in sizing up a situation and providing Skipper with all the data he needs to make a plan. Honest to a fault, Kowalski can always be counted on to provide up-to-the-minute information . . . even if some of that information isn't always helpful!

STRENGTHS

- Photographic memory

- Highly intelligent, yet sensitive

- Problem-solving skills

Kowalski's True but Unhelpful Comments

"Ninety-five percent certain we're still doomed."

"I'm not sure they're the ones that are trapped, sir."

"Brilliant move, Skipper, but now we seem to be outside the plane."

RICO, the Brawn

Rico is the wild card of the group, the go-to penguin when the craziest option has actually become the best solution. Because he's been known to swallow anything in his path (like snow globes), he can always vomit up exactly what you didn't even know you needed. Plus, when it comes to destroying things, whether it's a seat cushion or a secret lab, there's no one better!

STRENGTHS

- Regurgitating

- Having just what's needed

- Unfazed in the face of danger

Packed and Ready to Go!

Rico always keeps useful items tucked away in his tummy in case the penguins are ever in a jam. Here are some of the things Rico might swallow and store away for a secret mission:

- Binoculars   - Tape recorders   - DVDs   - Bags of Cheezy Dibbles

PRIVATE, the Rookie

The youngest member of the team, Private is prized for his unwavering optimism, bravery, and loyalty. Raised by his fellow teammates, Private yearns to prove to Skipper that he's more than just a secretary and mascot. He wants to become a valuable member of the team.

STRENGTHS

Believes in the impossible

Boosting team morale

Executing Skipper's plans

Private's Rules to Live By

- Never interrupt analogies
- No lollygagging or regular gagging
- Don't press strange buttons

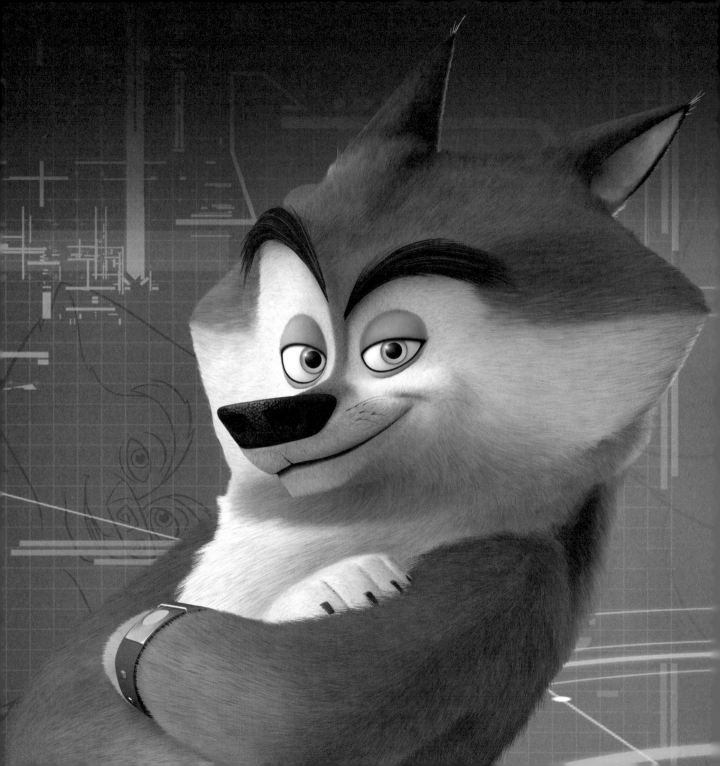

AGENT CLASSIFIED

His name is classified, not "Classified," but good luck trying to get the penguins to understand that! Agent Classified is the leader of the North Wind, an elite, undercover, interspecies task force dedicated to helping animals who can't help themselves. An expertly trained secret agent, Classified relies on attention to detail, protocol, and high-tech gadgetry to get answers . . . though they're not always the right ones!

STRENGTHS

- Using cool spy gadgets
- Making (overly) complicated plans
- Directing his team

Classified's Catchphrases

"Leave this to the professionals."

"I give the orders around here."

"My name isn't Classified. It's classified."

THE NORTH WIND

EVA

An intelligence analyst for the North Wind, Eva is a snowy owl with brains, beauty, and a killer instinct. Eva is quiet and goal-oriented—when she has her eye on something, you don't want to get in her way!

SHORT FUSE

This baby seal may look adorable, but he is an explosives expert who's a force to be reckoned with. And with his touchy temper, "Short Fuse" easily lives up to his name.

Words from the North Wind

"No one breaks the Wind."

"You are now under the protection of the North Wind. You're welcome."

CORPORAL

At eight feet tall and more than a thousand pounds, Corporal is the muscle behind the North Wind. But looks can be deceiving. This huge bear has a soft spot for all things cute and cuddly, especially penguins!

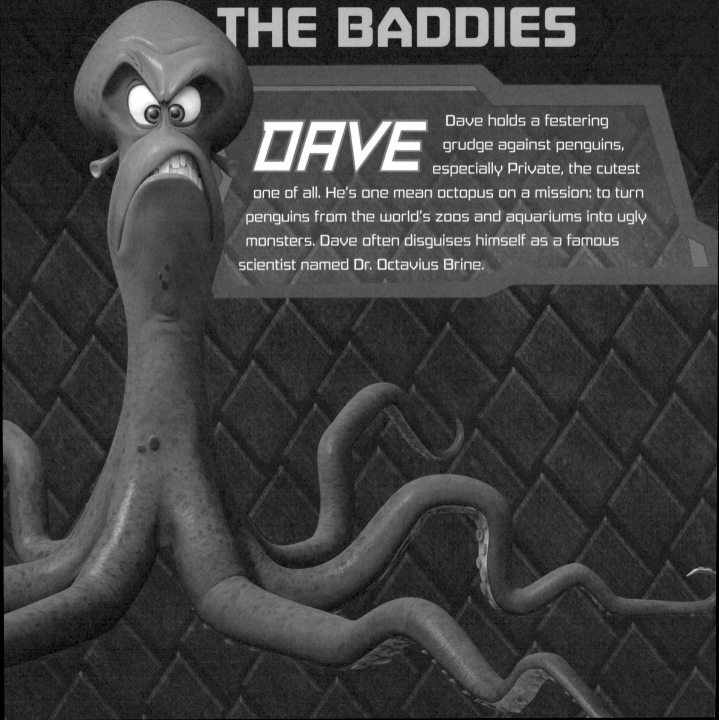

THE BADDIES

DAVE

Dave holds a festering grudge against penguins, especially Private, the cutest one of all. He's one mean octopus on a mission: to turn penguins from the world's zoos and aquariums into ugly monsters. Dave often disguises himself as a famous scientist named Dr. Octavius Brine.

Dave's Sob Story

Dave didn't start out as an evil mastermind. A long time ago, he was just an octopus at the New York Zoo. Sure, he could squeeze himself into a jar, but the visitors at the zoo didn't care. All they cared about were the cute and cuddly penguins. Soon, Dave found himself out on the street with the rest of the garbage. The same thing happened at the next zoo, and the one after that, and even at aquariums. After years of being ignored because everyone just loves penguins, Dave vowed to get revenge.

Dave's Henchmen

Dave employs henchmen who share his thirst for revenge against all penguins. Like Dave, they can change color to camouflage themselves, and since they don't have bones, they can squeeze into almost any space, no matter how small. Their ninja skills and strong suction grips make them a genuine threat to any foe.

Facts About Penguins

Itching for some intel about our fine, flippered heroes? Below are some fun facts about penguins.

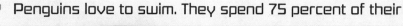

■ Emperor penguins have the most feathers of any bird—roughly a hundred feathers for every square inch keep them warm in freezing temperatures!

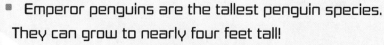

■ Penguins love to swim. They spend 75 percent of their time in the water.

■ Emperor penguins are the tallest penguin species. They can grow to nearly four feet tall!

■ Penguins like to stick together. Many penguin species will nest, feed, and swim in groups.

- Penguins can't fly, but their flippers are very useful for swimming.

- Penguins may not be able to breathe underwater, but some species can hold their breath for up to twenty minutes so they can dive down for food!

- Penguins have ears, but they're not visible like ours.

Dibble Me!

The penguins love Cheezy Dibbles so much, they even broke into Fort Knox to get them!

The boys also love hot dogs . . . even if, according to Skipper, they are only 17 percent actual dog.

Skipper adores potato chips, and if you say you don't love po-tay-toes, he'll say you're wrong.

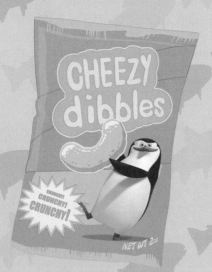

These chemically hazardous bits of puffed heaven are the penguins' all-time favorite treat!

Rico's always had a strange obsession with fish sticks. He won't tell us why, but we think they remind him of home.

Where's Private?

Can you find Private? He's munching on a Cheezy Dibble somewhere on this page!

Classified's Field Guide

If there's one thing Agent Classified is good at, it's knowing his surroundings. Check out the intel he's unearthed on some of the places the penguins have visited: Venice, Shanghai, and Antarctica!

Venice

- Venice is a city made up of 118 islands, 177 canals, and 416 bridges. Many people travel on gondolas, long thin boats that float on the city's canals.
- Venice is a very old city—it was first occupied in the mid-400s.
- The buildings in Venice weren't actually built on land. Instead the buildings were constructed on a series of wooden platforms.